MW01001585

RACHEL FRIEDMAN

and Eight Not-Perfect
Nights of Hanukkah

Also by Sarah Kapit

Rachel Friedman Breaks the Rules

Second Chance Summer

The Many Mysteries of the Finkel Family

Get a Grip, Vivy Cohen!

RACHEL FRIEDMAN

AND EIGHT NOT-PERFECT NIGHTS OF HANUKKAH

SARAH KAPIT

ILLUSTRATED BY GENEVIEVE KOTE

HENRY HOLT AND COMPANY

New York

Henry Holt and Company, *Publishers since 1866*
Henry Holt® is a registered trademark of Macmillan Publishing Group, LLC
120 Broadway, New York, NY 10271 • mackids.com

Text copyright © 2024 by Sarah Kapit. Illustrations copyright © 2024 by
Genevieve Kote. All rights reserved.

Our books may be purchased in bulk for promotional, educational, or business
use. Please contact your local bookseller or the Macmillan Corporate and
Premium Sales Department at (800) 221-7945 ext. 5442 or by email at
MacmillanSpecialMarkets@macmillan.com.

Library of Congress Cataloging-in-Publication Data is available.

First edition, 2024
Book design by Abby Granata
Printed in the United States of America by Lakeside Book Company,
Crawfordsville, Indiana

ISBN 978-1-250-88109-0 (hardcover)
1   3   5   7   9   10   8   6   4   2

ISBN 978-1-250-88107-6 (paperback)
1   3   5   7   9   10   8   6   4   2

To Dad

CHAPTER 1

The Best Holiday Ever?

Today is turning out to be an extra-fabulous day. In just a few hours, winter break is starting! That means almost two whole weeks with no school. I am so excited I can hardly stand it. But first I need to finish my drawing for art class.

I look over what I've made so far, and

my smile gets bigger and bigger. Ms. Ray told us to draw our favorite winter holiday traditions. So I made a drawing of my very favorite holiday: Hanukkah.

In the drawing, my entire family—me, my dad, my big brother, Aaron, and my cat, Cookie—stand by the counter while we light the menorah. Of course, in real life, we would never let Cookie go near the menorah. But I wanted to draw her anyway. She is a very important part of the family.

There is only one problem with my drawing. The space next to the menorah is empty, and that's boring. I decide to draw a plate of nice, hot latkes in the empty space. I like to eat my latkes with sour cream on top, but Aaron thinks they taste better with applesauce. Aaron and I disagree about a lot of things, but I'm happy to let him be wrong about this one. More sour cream for me!

I also draw a dreidel spinning because every year I play with dreidels. Now my artwork has all the biggest Hanukkah traditions! It really is perfect. I bounce up and down in my chair.

Since I'm done, I look over at the boy next to me. His name is Mason, and he's drawn a picture of a gigantic Christmas tree with a star on top.

"Nice drawing!" I tell him.

I don't know Mason very well because he just moved here, but I want to be nice. Maybe he can be a new friend.

Mason should say "thanks," because that is the polite thing to do when someone says a nice thing. But he doesn't. He just looks over at my drawing.

"You didn't make a Christmas tree," he says.

Well, duh! Of course I didn't draw a Christmas tree. Why did he say something so obvious? Even though he's asking a stupid question, I am going to keep on being nice to him anyway.

"I don't celebrate Christmas," I explain. "My family is Jewish, and we celebrate Hanukkah."

Really, Mason should already know this. We learned all about holidays this month, and I talked to the class about how my family celebrates Hanukkah. Maybe he wasn't paying attention, though. I sometimes have trouble paying attention in class, too.

He frowns. I don't know what he's frowning about. My drawing? The idea of Hanukkah? That's just silly! Hanukkah is the bestest holiday in the whole world. Much better than Christmas. *Obviously!*

"So you don't have a Christmas tree at all? Or stockings and sugar cookies?" Mason asks.

There he goes, talking about Christmas

again! Now I'm starting to get annoyed. More than annoyed. I just *told* him we don't celebrate Christmas. Some Jewish people do, like my cousins. But I never have.

"No, we don't have a Christmas tree and stockings," I say. "But we do have a

menorah! And we eat jelly doughnuts, not sugar cookies. My dad makes the best ones."

"But why can't you celebrate Christmas?"

I play with my hands. "Because . . . because we don't."

That's not a very good answer. But Mason didn't ask a very good question!

"You're missing out. Christmas is the best holiday," he says.

He looks back at his own drawing. I want to go back to my drawing, too, but I can't. I'm too confused. I don't understand why Mason would say something so silly. Why does he think I'm missing out?

I am not missing out on anything!

CHAPTER 2

Waiting for Hanukkah

should be stupendously happy right now. Not only do I have two whole weeks off from school but the first night of Hanukkah is tomorrow. Tomorrow!

So I guess I am happy. But I am also a little bit mad. Mason was wrong. The most wrong person in the history of wrong. Hanukkah is

a great holiday. Even though I've never cele-
brated Christmas, I am sure that Hanukkah
is better than Christmas. I mean, Hanukkah
lasts for eight days and eight nights. Christmas is only one day! Eight days is better
than one. That is just a fact.

Take that, Mason!

Luckily, my best friend, Maya, is at my
house for an after-school playdate. Maya
always makes everything better.

My dad grins at us while he gets out
a bowl of pretzels for our snack. "Are you
excited about Hanukkah, girls?" he asks.

"YES!" we answer together.

"I can't believe it starts tomorrow," Maya
tells me while we start to munch on pretzels. "My moms already bought so much
chocolate gelt! I can't wait."

I bounce up and down in my chair.

"That's the best part! Well, besides the pre-sents. Obviously."

"Obviously!"

I look at Dad. "Did you get the race car yet?"

I want a race car for my doll *so much*.

Just to make sure that Dad knows, I made a picture of it and put it on the refrigerator with the words HANUKKAH GIFT FOR RACHEL in big letters.

"Maybe," Dad says. "Maybe not. You'll have to wait and see."

He looks at me and pretends to zip his lips up like a jacket. Annoying!

Still, I'm feeling so excited about Hanukkah and everything that I almost don't mind. Dad pats me on the back and goes off to do Dad things. I hope those things involve wrapping presents.

That's when Aaron walks into the room and grabs a fistful of pretzels.

"Hey, Maya," he says. "Hey, Rachey."

I scowl at him. He knows I don't like it when he calls me Rachey, but he does it anyway.

Maya smiles at him, though. She likes him for some reason. Maybe because he's actually nice to her.

"Are you excited about Hanukkah, Aaron?" she asks.

I expect my brother to say yes. I mean, what other answer is there? But instead, he just shrugs.

"Not really."

What?! I cannot believe he would say this. Cannot! Aaron and I don't agree on most things, but we always agree on Hanukkah. Most of the year, we fight all the time, but we put it aside on Hanukkah. Dad says it's a true Hanukkah miracle.

"What?" Maya and I say together.

Aaron shrugs again. Which is very, very annoying.

"I said what I said. You know, Hanukkah

isn't even an important holiday. I read about it."

Aaron is always talking about something that he read. He is a know-it-all like that.

I open my mouth to explain to him the bajillion reasons why he's wrong. But before I get the chance, he sprints out of there with his pretzels. Rude!

CHAPTER 3
Making a List

My brother is the worst. But it's not like I wanted to spend time with him anyway. Maya and I finish our snack before heading up to my room, because we have manners. We sprawl out on the floor together.

"I cannot believe how many people don't like Hanukkah!" I tell her. "First Mason and now Aaron."

Maya frowns. "Mason? What about him?"

So I explain all about what happened with my drawing. How he said that I'm "missing out."

"That's terrible!" Maya says. "He shouldn't feel sorry for us just because we don't celebrate Christmas. Why would he say something so mean?"

"I know! What's so great about Christmas, anyway?" I say in my grumpy voice.

Maya shrugs. "Well . . ."

"Well, what?" I demand.

"Well, it kind of does look like a lot of fun in the movies and on TV."

That's true. There are a bajillion movies and TV show episodes about Christmas. Plus seventy bajillion commercials about Christmas. On TV, Christmas *does* look pretty great. There's always lots of food, laughing, and singing. But Hanukkah has those things, too!

"Forget about Christmas," I say. "This year, we're going to have the best Hanukkah ever. Eight perfect nights."

Maya grins widely at me. "Totally!"

I immediately feel better. Yes! This is exactly what I need. After eight perfect nights of Hanukkah, Mason won't ever be able to say that I'm missing out. I'm not missing out on anything. He's the one who's missing out!

"We should make a plan," I declare. My dad is always talking about how plans make things happen. Blah, blah, blah. Normally I don't really bother with making plans. But this is important!

"What kind of a plan?" Maya asks.

The answer comes to me at once. "We should make a list! Eight super-fun things to do for eight days of Hanukkah."

"Oooh, yes!" Maya pulls out a notebook and pen from her bag. "Should we write everything down, so that it's official?"

I jump up and down. "Yes!"

The first few things on the list are easy. We want to eat lots and lots of latkes. We're going to do a dreidel-spinning contest. And we both want good presents. Maya wants

a new jewelry-making kit. I want the race car, obviously.

So, that's three things already. Now we just need five more.

"What about the Lego menorah?" Maya asks. "You guys always do that."

Yes! Our family always makes a gigantic Lego menorah for the front porch. Aaron started doing it when I was just a baby, and now it's our tradition. Every year it looks a little different—but it's always fantabulous.

"Add it to the list," I say.

There are a lot of super-fun Hanukkah things we do every year, so it isn't hard to come up with ideas. We even want to start a brand-new tradition—ice-skating! Really, we should be in charge of every holiday.

In the end, we come up with a list of seven awesome things:

1. Cook latkes and eat them. (Be sure to add lots of sour cream!)
2. Do a dreidel-spinning contest. (Eat lots of gelt after!)
3. Build the best Lego menorah ever. (Even bigger than last year's.)
4. Make a Snow Maccabee. (Don't forget to add the sword!)
5. Go ice-skating. (A new Hanukkah tradition!)
6. Sing Hanukkah songs in the park. (The good ones only.)
7. Get fabulous presents. (Plus, start playing with them.)

I frown. Coming up with seven things was easy, but now I don't know what to do for number eight. The last number on the list can't be just anything. It should be superspecial, to finish off a superspecial holiday. This Hanukkah needs to be better than all the other Hanukkahs.

"Maybe we can watch that old cartoon about Hanukkah?" Maya suggests.

"Boring!" I say. "We've seen that like a million times already."

Maya makes a not-happy face back at me. "Raaachel. Don't be like this. We have to come up with something!"

"We have to come up with the perfect thing," I correct her. "Eight perfect nights, remember?"

Maya looks like she wants to argue with me, but she doesn't. She just bites her lip.

"Okay. Fine. How about we leave number eight blank? Until we find the perfect thing."

I wish I knew the perfect number eight right now! I don't want to wait. But I guess Maya is right. So I go back to the list and write:

8. ???

CHAPTER 4

Build a Lego Menorah

After Maya and I make our list, I feel much better about everything. Hanukkah is always fabulous, but this year it's going to be even better than fabulous. It will be the *most* fabulous.

Maya goes home for dinner. But I decide to start working on one of the most important things on the list: building a Lego menorah.

Of course, I'll need Aaron's help. I am talented at many things: gymnastics, drawing, and coming up with great ideas. But Aaron is better than me at building things with Legos.

I know he said he's not doing Hanukkah this year, but I don't believe him. Once I start doing Hanukkah-y things, he'll join in. I know he will.

I pound on the door to his room. When he doesn't answer, I go in anyway.

"We need to build the menorah!" I announce.

Aaron doesn't even look up from his computer. So annoying! I don't know what he's doing, but it can't possibly be more important than building the Lego menorah.

"The menorah's probably in one of the cabinets," he says.

I roll my eyes. We do have a menorah for lighting candles, and it's very pretty, but I don't mean that one.

"Not that menorah. I mean the Lego menorah. For the front yard."

I don't know why I need to explain this to him, but maybe all that looking at the computer has made Aaron's memory get funny.

"I told you," he says. "I'm not doing Hanukkah stuff this year. Don't feel like it."

"But *why* don't you feel like it?" I ask him. Because, really, I have got to know.

My brother lets out a long sigh. "I'm too old for Lego menorahs. That stuff was fun when I was a kid, but now I have better things to do with my time."

I put my hands on my hips. "Oh yeah? And what do you have to do that's so important?"

Aaron likes to read comic books and play video games with his friends. How can that possibly be more important than our Lego menorah? It doesn't make any sense.

"Just things." He waves around the room. As if that means anything. Then he turns back to the computer. "If you want a Lego menorah so much, you can build it yourself."

"I will!"

I clench my teeth and march out of the room. Maybe Aaron is being horrible, but I still have my plan.

CHAPTER 5

The Problem with Legos

The next morning, I wake up with a mission. I am going to make the best Lego menorah ever, without Aaron. I don't need him. Not even a little bit!

He'll be sorry when he sees what a great job I do.

Besides, I have the bestest best friend in

the entire world to help. Maya lives on the same street as me, so she can get here right away. I send off a text: *LEGO MENORAH TIME!!!!*

While I wait for a response, I pace in my room.

Finally, a new message appears: *Can't.*

A sick-face emoji pops up below the word.

I stare at my phone. Maya can't come over?!

I'm sick. Not too bad, but I don't want you to get sick, too.

I guess that makes sense. Even though it really, really stinks for both of us. *Hope you get better soon*, I tell her.

Maybe she'll get better before Hanukkah ends and we can still do the stuff on our list. But maybe not. I

bite my lip. Do I really have to do every-thing all by myself?

For a moment, I feel very sad. But I try to shake it off. I can do this. I am going to have the best Hanukkah ever, and I am not going to let anything stand in my way. I'll build the Lego menorah myself.

Even if getting the Legos from the base-ment by myself takes a really long time.

I put on a warm coat and hat before going

outside. Then I dump the Legos on the front porch and look at them. There are twenty bazillion Legos. Suddenly I realize how hard it's going to be to make this menorah.

If Aaron were here, he would know exactly what to do.

But Aaron isn't here. It's only me.

"I don't need him," I say to no one. Because I don't.

I try putting the Legos in different piles for each color, but that's boring. Aaron's the one who actually likes sorting Legos. So I start stacking the bricks right away. Maybe my menorah isn't going to look exactly like Aaron's would, but that's okay. All I need to do is build the bottom of the menorah, eight stacks for the candles, plus one taller stack for the shammash. How hard could that be?

As it turns out: Hard! I build the base for

the menorah, then two candles, but when I start on the third, I realize that my stacks are uneven. No good. I tear my towers apart and start over again.

The front door opens, and Aaron wanders over. He watches me.

"Are you going to help?" I ask him.

I don't want to act like I need his help or anything, because I don't. Still, it would be nice.

He blinks. For a second, I'm pretty sure he's going to say yes. But instead, he shakes his head.

"Nope! Legos are for little kids, and so is Hanukkah." He gives me a big smile. "It's perfect for you, Rachey."

I stand up so fast that I accidentally knock over one of the Lego towers with my foot. "I am not a little kid! And Hanukkah is for everyone. You're just annoying."

Aaron shrugs and goes back inside the house. Good! I don't need him and his stupid anti-Hanukkah ideas here.

I go back to the menorah and frown. It doesn't look right.

Why is everything so hard?

I break the Lego candles apart and start over. I build one tower from blue Legos, and it looks pretty good. So I build another tower out of yellow bricks and a third from green. Then I go back to the blue.

I've got this!

I start on my eighth tower—the last candle. This one's going to be red. Except for one small problem.

There aren't any more red Legos. In fact, there aren't many Legos of any color.

My menorah only has seven and a half candles. Which means it's not a menorah.

I grind my teeth and look at my not-a-real menorah. I could try to fix it, maybe. But I'm just not in the mood. I take the whole thing apart so I don't have to keep looking at it. I shove the Legos back into the box.

So much for the perfect Hanukkah.

CHAPTER 6

A Snowy Hanukkah

I feel antsy for the rest of the morning. Why is Aaron acting like such a grump? Doesn't he know that he's ruining Hanukkah? I sure hope he's not going to be like this for all eight days. Especially since I don't have Maya.

But by the time afternoon rolls around, I start feeling a little better. Maybe Aaron is trying to ruin Hanukkah, but I will not let him. Not only is tonight the first night of Hanukkah but it's also Latke Night! We always do latkes on the first night. Dad and I can cook lots of delicious latkes without Aaron. And since I'm going to be making them, I'll take all the crispiest ones for myself. That will show him!

Then things get even better: Snow starts falling right before dinner! This must mean it's going to be an extra-special Hanukkah after all. Sure, the original Hanukkah story doesn't have snow, because it happened in the desert and everything. But that doesn't matter. Snow on Hanukkah means a fantabulous Hanukkah. I know it.

After I feed Cookie, I go off to find Dad. He's reading a book in the living room.

When he sees me, he gives me a great big smile.

"It's latke time!" I remind him.

He claps his hands. "Right you are, Rachel! Let's get started."

We go into the kitchen. Dad opens the refrigerator and groans.

Uh-oh.

"Rachey," he says. "I think we have a small problem, kiddo."

A problem? How can there possibly be a problem with latkes?

Frowning, I bounce over to him. Dad pats me on the shoulder.

"I'm so sorry, hon. But it looks like I forgot to buy the potatoes," he says.

That is not a small problem. That is a big, big problem. I can't believe it!

"What?" I yelp. "How could you forget the potatoes?"

Dad runs a hand through his hair. "I can't believe it. I bought onions and eggs and flour and everything else for latkes, but . . . I forgot the potatoes. I'm sorry."

If there's one thing that's true about

latkes, it's this: Latkes need to have potatoes. There's just no way around it.

I look in the fridge. Maybe Dad's wrong.
Maybe there is a bag of potatoes hiding
somewhere. I look and I look. But he's right.
Not a single potato to be found.

I chew on my lip. "Can't we go out and
get some potatoes?"

Dad glances out the window. Snow is

falling even harder now. I can hardly see the houses across the street because everything is covered in a flurry of white. Dad frowns.

"I want to, honey-bear. But driving to the grocery store in the snow is going to take forever. Plus, it could get dangerous."

He's right. I know he's right. But I still don't like it.

"We always have latkes on the first night!" I remind him.

"I know, I know. But they're going to taste just as good on the second or third night, okay? It's something to look forward to."

What he says makes sense, though I'm still not happy about it. Frowning, I think back to my list. I haven't managed to do a single thing on it today. Now even Latke Night isn't happening thanks to snow and no potatoes. Maybe snow on Hanukkah isn't such a great thing after all.

"I guess we can do latkes another night," I say.

If Dad remembers to get potatoes, that is. But I don't say that part out loud.

"Thanks for understanding, Rachey." Dad opens the freezer. "How about some pizza for dinner? You love pizza."

I do. But pizza on Hanukkah? Something about it just doesn't feel right.

It's not like there's much of a choice, though, so I nod.

Dad smiles at me. "Pizza it is."

CHAPTER 7

A Pizza-licious Night

P izza for Hanukkah is weird. I still think that. But pizza tastes good on any night. And not only is the pizza extra-cheesy but it also has peppers. Yum! I eat two slices and start on a third.

"The whole pizza-on-Hanukkah thing has been a success, don't you think?" Dad says.

I would answer, but my mouth is full of cheesy goodness. Aaron says "yeah" in between bites.

Once we finish, Dad claps. "Menorah time!" he announces.

I perk up. Lighting the menorah wasn't on my list of eight super-fun things, but it's still part of Hanukkah. Dad says it's the most important part, and I guess he's right. (Even though it's not the most fun.)

Dad pulls out a brand-new box of Hanukkah candles while Aaron moves the menorah to the table.

"Did you know that this isn't really a menorah?" Aaron says. "The correct term is *hanukkiah*. A real menorah only has seven candles."

I make a face at him. Really, what does it matter if we call it a menorah or a hanukkiah? It's just a name! Our rabbi always says that actions are more important than using the right words all the time.

I want to tell Aaron to stop being such a know-it-all, but Dad speaks first. "Thank you for teaching us something new, Aaron," he says. "Now, who would like to light the menorah tonight?"

"Hanukkiah," Aaron corrects.

"I want to do it. I want to!" I say at once, ignoring Aaron.

I expect Aaron to argue with me about it, but he doesn't. So at least there's that.

"Excellent, Rachey," Dad says.

He lights a match because I'm not allowed to use matches. Next, he uses the match to light the shammash—the candle

that lights all the other candles. He hands the shammash to me.

I take a deep breath and light the very first candle on the menorah. (I'm still calling it a menorah, not a hanukkiah. Take that, Aaron!)

Since it's the first night, I only have to light one candle. Together, we sing the first prayer: "Baruch atah Adonai, Eloheinu Melech Ha'olam . . ."

After we finish, we sing the second prayer, plus the third prayer that's only for the first night. Dad smiles. He squeezes me and Aaron at the same time.

"Happy Hanukkah, crew!" he says.

"Happy Hanukkah," we say back.

Dad moves the menorah up to the

counter. I always feel a little nervous that Cookie might go up and knock it over, but Dad says she's too smart.

Now that lighting the menorah is done, only one part of Hanukkah is left for tonight. A very, very important part.

"Are we going to do presents?" I ask, hopping in place.

Dad scratches his chin. "I'm sorry, but I think the presents ended up in the same place as the potatoes."

What? No!

Dad looks at my face and then laughs. "Just kidding, Rachey. Of course we're going to do presents."

"Yay, yay, and yay!" I start dancing in the kitchen.

Dad goes off to wherever he hides the presents. He is very good at hiding them. I know because I tried to look this afternoon,

but I couldn't find anything.

I wonder what I'm going to get tonight. Dad always gives the best presents on the first night of Hanukkah and the last. Maybe tonight I'll get my race car!

When he comes back, Dad hands me a gift wrapped in blue-and-silver paper. The present looks thin and soft. Not at all like a race car box.

I try not to feel disappointed, but I kind of do.

But when I rip the wrapping open, I squeal. No, it's not a race car. But it is a new leotard for gymnastics. Even better, it's the same sparkly purple leotard that Holly Luna sometimes wears. Holly is my favorite gymnast in the whole world. Now I get to wear a leotard that looks just like hers! I'm going to be even better at gymnastics thanks to this leotard.

I smile at Dad. "Thank you, thank you, thank you!"

He winks at me.

"Just in time for your next competition, right?"

"I am going to be perfect!" I say.

Aaron is really happy with his present, too. Dad gave him a gift card to buy new video games, which is kind of a boring present if you ask me. But that's what Aaron

likes. I guess he still wants to get presents, even if he did go through that whole thing about how Hanukkah isn't important. Now, that is what I call contradicting yourself.

"I know things didn't go exactly as planned, but I think we can count the first night of Hanukkah as a success," Dad says.

He's right. The first night of Hanukkah was very, very good. Even though it would have been *perfect* if we'd just had latkes.

Also, I still need to come up with number eight for the list.

CHAPTER 8

Do You Want to Build a Snow Maccabee?

When I wake up and look outside the window, the whole world is white. And the snow has stopped falling. This can only mean one thing: It is time to make a Snow Maccabee!

I get dressed super fast so I can go outside right away. Aaron is already up, lounging on the couch with his phone.

I chew on my lip. Aaron has been a total grump for Hanukkah so far. But this is a snow day! Obviously he is going to go outside to play with me. Because that's what we do on snow days.

"Get off your butt!" I tell him. "It's time to go build a Snow Maccabee."

Aaron points to a mug on the coffee table. "*I* am enjoying my hot chocolate, thank you very much. Go out in the cold to build a snowman? No thanks."

"It's not a snowman. It's a Snow Maccabee! For Hanukkah."

"Whatever you call it, I'm not going outside."

Ugh! Of course Aaron is going to be difficult again. But I make myself stand tall and give him a look. Hopefully, the look says "You are being very annoying, and I am tired of it."

"Well, I am going to have fun. Be boring if you want."

I really wish I could go over and get Maya. She would help me make the best

Snow Maccabee ever. But I guess I'll just have to do it myself.

I grab my winter coat and snow boots before going outside. Even with my coat, the cold still takes me by surprise. I think about going back inside, just for a moment.

But then I remember Mason and the list and Aaron and how terrible he's being. I have to prove that Hanukkah is the best holiday ever. So I march through the snow. Dad hasn't even shoveled the snow off the porch yet, which makes the journey to the front lawn even more exciting. And maybe just a little bit dangerous.

I smile when I reach the field of snow that now covers our yard. This is going to be so great! A few years ago, we had a Hanukkah snowstorm. That's when I came up with the idea of building a Snow Maccabee. A Snow Maccabee looks like a snowman, except that I decorate it with a cape and a fake sword. Really, it's much better than just a boring old snowman.

The Maccabees were a bunch of Jewish people. They are the heroes of the Hanukkah story. They fought against the Greeks a really, really long time ago. The Greek rulers told Jewish people they should stop being Jewish. Which was a totally and completely terrible thing to do. But the Maccabee soldiers beat the Greeks! And then they lit the menorah! The oil lasted for eight whole days, even though they only had enough for one day. Which is a miracle. That's why we celebrate Hanukkah. And now I am going to make a Snow Maccabee.

Except for one small problem. There isn't that much snow. Even though it sure felt like a lot of snow fell yesterday, it's probably only three or four inches deep.

Okay, fine. I can still do this. I start scooping up snow. I make a ball for the base of the Snow Maccabee, and then another ball. They're a little lopsided, but that's okay. I'm the one who invented Snow Maccabees. So if I say that they're funny-looking, then it must be true.

I try to make a third ball for the Snow Maccabee's head, but my hands are getting cold even with my gloves on. I don't really

feel like scraping up enough snow for the head. Oh well. Maybe this is a short Snow Maccabee.

Still, it doesn't look right. And that doesn't feel right to me.

I try not to think about it. I give the Snow Maccabee tree branches for arms and a pine cone nose. I'll figure out the eyes and mouth later. Now it's time to go inside so I can get the cape and sword. Did the real Maccabees wear capes? I'm not sure, but capes look cool. So that's what I'm doing.

I really do want to finish the Snow Maccabee. But when I get inside, everything feels so nice and warm. Dad has started up a fire in the fireplace. He hands me a mug of hot chocolate. The smell is so good that I grab it right away and start to drink.

By the time I'm done with my hot chocolate, I don't feel like going out into the snow again. The Snow Maccabee can wait until later.

Besides . . . I have to admit something: Doing Hanukkah alone just isn't that much fun.

CHAPTER 9

Spin the Dreidels

I decide that I can check off "Make a Snow Maccabee" on the list, even if I didn't finish it. Close enough! So that's one thing already done. And tonight I am going to do something else: the dreidel-spinning contest. The only problem is that I don't have someone to compete against. I can't count on Aaron to do Hanukkah things with me.

I'll just have to figure it out.

Dinner is not-latkes again. We still don't have any potatoes. My present is a book. Which is nice, I guess, but where's the race car?

At least there are six nights left. On one of those nights there will be latkes and a race car. There *has* to be.

After we light the candles, I decide to do my dreidel-spinning contest. (Even if it's not really a contest, since I'm the only one doing it.) I sit down on the living room floor, in the corner where there isn't any rug. This is the best dreidel-spinning place in the house.

Aaron sits on the couch with his legs stretched out. He also got a book for his present, and now he's reading it.

"I am spinning the dreidels!" I announce.

Aaron looks up from his book. "By your-self?"

"Yeah. Since you don't want to do Hanukkah."

He shifts on the couch, and I start to think maybe he'll join me on the floor after all. But he doesn't.

"Whatever," Aaron says before return-ing to his book.

Ugh. I need to just forget about him.

I open the box and take out my very favorite dreidel. It's made out of wood, with Hebrew letters carved into it. Each letter is a different color. The four letters are *nun*, *gimel*, *hey*, and *shin*. That's like the letters *N*, *G*, and *H* in English, plus the *shh* sound for shin.

In the usual game, you put a bowl of pennies or chocolate gelt coins in the middle of the floor. Then you spin the dreidel. Depending on what letter the dreidel lands on, you have to either take coins from the bowl or put them back. Or possibly nothing happens if you spin nun.

But here's the thing about the dreidel game. It is so, so boring. The entire game is just luck, and I don't like that. I want to win! I can't play the dreidel game for more than ten minutes before I start getting tired of it. That's why I invented the dreidel-spinning contest.

The rules of the dreidel-spinning contest are simple. You have to spin as many dreidels as you can, all at the same time. Last year, Aaron got seven at once! He is really good at this game, and that's annoying. At least I won't have to compete with him this year.

I've never managed to spin more than four dreidels at a time, but I choose eight more dreidels from the box. Just in case. I make sure to pick the dreidels that look the spinniest.

Before I begin, I take a deep breath. Then I spin the first dreidel. It totters to the floor in two seconds. I guess my dreidel-spinning skills are out of practice. So I spin the one dreidel for a bit, to get the feel of things.

Now it's time to begin for real. I spin one dreidel. Yes! I spin another. That's two. But as I start up on number three, the first dreidel falls down. Oh no!

This game is really hard. But that's all the more reason why I have to do it.

After ten minutes, I manage to get three

dreidels spinning at once. But I struggle to get to four. Why? What am I doing wrong?

Across the room, Aaron puts his book down. He stares at me and sighs.

"You're not doing this right," he says.

That takes some nerve! My grandma would say he's showing a lot of chutzpah. Aaron won't join in my contest, but now he wants to criticize me? I cross my arms over my chest.

"If you're so great, then you do it!" I tell him.

I totally expect him to scowl at me and return to his book, like he's been doing the whole night. But he doesn't. Instead, he gets up from the couch and plops himself next to me on the floor.

"Spinning a dreidel is all about the fingers," he explains.

He flicks a dreidel, and it starts spinning super fast. Like magic, Aaron makes one dreidel spin, then another, and another, and pretty soon there are six going at once.

When he finishes, I clap. Aaron may be annoying, but I have to respect his skill. At least when it comes to dreidels.

I'm about to give up on it. There is no way I can beat Aaron at this contest. But he turns to me and smiles.

"You can do it, too, Rachey."

So I give it another try. I copy the way Aaron moves his fingers. I don't get it perfect, but my dreidel is spinning faster. I spin one dreidel, then three, then four. I start working on number five when all the dreidels crash down at once.

Not because I did anything wrong. But because someone has knocked them over.

Cookie looks up at me with her big, wide eyes. She has no idea that she just messed up the dreidel spinning.

"Cookie! Can't you see I'm spinning dreidels?" I scold her.

I don't want to be mad at my cat, but maybe I am, just a little.

Of course, Cookie only meows at me. Well, now I can't be mad at all. Dreidel-spinning contests just aren't very important to cats.

I give her a pat on the head. "Good girl," I say in my very sweetest voice. "Even though I was about to beat Aaron and you ruined it."

Aaron laughs at me. "Yeah, I don't think so, Rachey."

"I totally was!" I insist.

I was not going to beat him, and we both know it. But he doesn't point that out, which is nice of him. And also weird.

Still, as I put away the dreidels, I realize

something. A very, very important something. Aaron did a Hanukkah thing with me! Even if he is annoying, I'm glad that he did.

Now I know the eighth thing to put on my list: *Get Aaron to admit that Hanukkah is fun.*

CHAPTER 10

A Trip to the Park

The next few days of Hanukkah go by, and I still haven't finished most of the things on my list. Not even the latkes! Dad says we'll do them on the last night. I just hope he doesn't forget the potatoes again. I need to prove to Mason and everyone else that Hanukkah is awesome, and I can't do that without latkes!

Today is the fifth day, and Dad took off from work for "family time." That means it's the perfect chance to do another thing on my list.

So when Dad asks me and Aaron what we want to do, I know my answer right away. "Skating! Please, pretty, pretty please! And also, please?"

Dad looks at Aaron. I am not surprised when Aaron makes one of his faces. Again.

"Do we have to?" he complains. "I'm not a sports type like Rachel, you know."

"Sure, but you don't need to be sportsy to enjoy a few hours of skating." Dad rubs his forehead. "How about this? We skate in the morning, and then in the afternoon we go to the science museum."

"I guess that works," Aaron says. But he sounds like someone who just agreed to eat a jar full of rotten gefilte fish.

My whole mission to get Aaron to admit that Hanukkah is fun seems like it might be kind of hard. But that's okay! There is nothing in the whole world that I can't do.

When we arrive at the park, everything is still covered in Christmas decorations. Even though Christmas was three whole days ago. I don't see any Hanukkah decorations at all. I'm used to this. But I can't help but frown.

Why is everything always Christmas, Christmas, Christmas for two months a year?

"Looks like someone forgot that Christmas is over," Aaron says.

Finally, we agree on something.

"I know!" I say. "Why can't the park have decorations for other holidays, too?"

Aaron shrugs. "People really like Christmas, I guess."

I think back to Mason and all the things he said to me. The memory of it makes me mad. Christmas isn't a better holiday just because more people celebrate it or because there's Christmas stuff everywhere! Hanukkah is still better, and I am going to prove it.

Even if things haven't gone exactly to plan so far.

Dad squeezes me on the shoulder. "I felt left out around Christmas when I was your age, too. It can be a little strange when so many people are celebrating a holiday and you aren't."

"I don't feel left out!" I protest. Except I kind of do. "Well, maybe I do. Just a little bit. But it's only because the Christmas stuff is everywhere!"

"Yeah, it can be annoying," Dad agrees. "I try to focus on how pretty the lights are and not think so much about that other stuff, but you're right. There should be more decorations for Hanukkah and Kwanzaa and every other holiday. Sometimes the world isn't fair."

At least my dad agrees with me. Feeling a bit better about the whole thing, I grab my ice skates and grin at Dad and Aaron. "Beat you to the rink!" I shout.

CHAPTER 11
At Top Speed

Gymnastics is my sport, but I also love skating. Love it! I step on the ice the very moment I finish tying up the laces to my skates.

I'm a little wobbly at first, since it's been so long since I've skated. But I remember how to do everything pretty quick, and soon I'm whizzing around the rink. The wind flaps against my face, and my hair starts to slip out of its ponytail. I don't mind. I am skating!

When I finish my second lap, I notice Dad. He's at the edge of the rink, moving so slowly that he might as well be standing still. I race over to him.

"Da-ad! You can go faster than that."

He smiles at me but looks a little nervous. Like he really can't work up the energy to smile right now.

"I don't know about that, honey-bear," he says. "You might not have noticed, but your dad is old."

Silly Dad! I shake my head at him. "You're not as old as Grandma, and *she* skates faster than you do."

Dad laughs. "All right, all right. You caught me. I guess I don't want to fall."

"If you fall, you can just get back up again!" I tell him, because *duh*. "That's what Coach Kayla always says. You have to go for it, Dad."

Dad looks around the ice and then nods. "Well, I can't question the wisdom of Coach Kayla. How about you hold my hand, Rachey?"

I grab Dad's hand, and together we skate around the rink. While I don't go as fast as I normally would, at least Dad is no longer moving at the speed of a sleepy turtle.

I really wish Maya were here, just like we'd planned. We would have so much fun together. I know it. But she told me in a text that she doesn't want to risk passing on germs to anyone, even though she's feeling better. Still, even without Maya, things are almost fantabulous.

The only problem is my brother. *Again.* Instead of skating like someone who actually wants to have fun, he's sitting on a bench outside the rink. And he's on his phone. *Again.*

"Come on!" I call over to him. "You have to join the Hanukkah spirit!"

"Skating has nothing to do with Hanukkah," he grumbles. "The original story happened in the desert."

"I *know* that," I say. Ugh! The way Aaron acts sometimes, it's like he thinks I don't know anything about anything. But I go to Hebrew school, and sometimes I even pay attention. "In case you didn't notice, we're not in the desert. We're in New Jersey, where there is ice and snow! Why do you not like having fun?"

Aaron fidgets with his hands, and glances at the ice skates sitting next to him. "I don't know . . ."

"Come on! Unless you think you can't do it," I say.

81

Of course Aaron knows how to skate. I only said that to get him riled up, as Dad would say. And it works.

He starts shoving his skates on his feet. "Fine. But only so I can race you. And beat you."

"You are not going to beat me!" I say.

Aaron laughs. But he gets on the ice.

CHAPTER 12

On Thin Ice

"Dad is the judge," I say once Aaron makes it to the center of the rink. "He can be fair and . . . what's the word for it? Impactful?"

Aaron rolls his eyes. "Impartial. The word you mean is *impartial*."

"Whatever! Anyway, the rules are, we go from one end of the rink to the other. And no cheating!"

I had to add that part, because Aaron can be a terrible, horrible cheater.

"How would I even cheat at a race?" Aaron asks.

I don't answer. Instead, I skate toward the place where the race is going to begin. Aaron catches up with me a moment later.

"We go when I count to three," he says.

"What?" I demand. "Why do you get to do the count?"

He rolls his eyes. "Like it even matters."

"It matters!"

"Fine," he says. "We'll count together."

And we do.

"One . . . ," we chant.

I dig my skates into the ice.

"Two . . . THREE!"

I take off.

I'm gliding forward at top speed. But so

is Aaron. I have quicker feet, but Aaron's legs are longer. A lot longer. Pretty soon, he's flown ahead of me. I can see his ear-muffs getting farther and farther away.

No! I can't let him win.

I bend down. Maybe Aaron is taller than me, but there are good things about being short. I allow the wind to carry me, and soon we're almost neck and neck.

"Hello!" I say to him. "Nice to see you here."

"Even nicer to say goodbye," Aaron tells me.

We're about ten feet away from Dad. He waves his arm at the finishing point. I take a deep breath. My legs are tired, but

I force them to go on anyway. I'm almost there!

Aaron slides across the finish line about five seconds before me. He turns and grins as I skate by.

"I guess maybe I can skate a little," he says.

"You only won because you're taller!" I protest.

"Wow, Rachey. You sure are good at being a sore loser."

I stick my tongue out at him.

Dad shakes his head. "Cut it out, crew." He wobbles in his skates. "I think I've reached my limit for today. I'm getting off the ice. Try not to kill each other without me, please."

"I can babysit Rachel," Aaron promises while Dad takes tiny steps toward the edge of the rink.

He's only teasing me, but I don't like it. Aaron is *not* my babysitter. I want to come up with a smart response. But just as I open my mouth to deliver it, I notice something. Aaron isn't paying attention to me at all anymore. He's looking at someone else—a red-headed girl in a green jacket. She's skating with a bunch of other girls. They all look like they're close to Aaron's age.

"Hi, Aaron!" the girl says. "Wow. I didn't expect to see you here."

It takes Aaron a long time to respond, and when he does he sounds kind of weird. Squeaky. "H-hi, Miranda," he says. "Um. Nice to see you. Hi."

One of Miranda's friends giggles and pokes her in the ribs. Aaron stares at his skates. Well, all of this is super boring. I don't know these girls, and obviously they're not Aaron's friends if he can't find anything to say to them other than "Um. Nice to see you. Hi."

This is supposed to be family time. Aaron should pay attention to me. I nudge him on the shoulder.

"Race you one more time!" I say.

He doesn't respond, so I grab him and pull on his arm. Because I'm here and he needs to know it.

But I guess this surprises him. Because Aaron falls over onto the ice, taking me with him.

CHAPTER 13

The Worst Day of Hanukkah

"**B**lech! Argh!" Aaron says. Or at least that's close to what he says. It's kind of hard to understand the sounds he's making.

"Oh no!" I say. "Ack!"

When I said before that falling wasn't so bad, I had forgotten something very, very important. I fall all the time when I do gymnastics. But in gymnastics, there's always a nice, soft mat to catch me. Now there's just cold, hard ice. My butt stings with the cold and soreness.

I think maybe I don't love ice-skating. At least not right now.

I force myself to get up. The ice feels cold and icky on my hands, but at least I manage to move. That's when I look at Aaron.

He is not getting up. In fact, he has curled into himself and is now moaning.

"Aaron!" Miranda cries. "Are you okay?"

He speaks through gritted teeth. "I'm fine. Completely and totally fine."

Only he isn't. Miranda and one of her friends have to help him off the ice because his leg is so hurt. He doesn't even look at me as he hobbles away.

"I'm sorry," I say out loud. "I am so, so sorry. The sorriest."

I don't know if he even hears me, but I have to say it.

The moment Aaron gets off the ice, Dad announces that we're going to the emergency room so a doctor can look at Aaron's leg. Ice-skating is over. And it's all my fault.

_ll____ll_

The doctor says that Aaron broke his leg. Now he's walking with crutches and a great big cast.

"I'm sorry. I didn't mean to hurt you," I say on our way home from the hospital. I've said this about a bajillion times, but it couldn't hurt to say it a bajillion and one.

Aaron just grunts. Dad looks over at me.

"I think you need to give Aaron some

time," he says in a whisper. "His leg is hurting, and he's embarrassed."

"Huh? Why is he embarrassed?" I wonder out loud.

After all, it's not like Aaron is to blame for falling. That was me. I bite my lip so hard it hurts.

When Dad answers me, he whispers again: "Falling in front of the girl he likes was hard for him."

At first I don't understand what Dad means, but then I get it. *Oh*. Aaron likes Miranda the redhead. That's why he acted so weird around her. And that's why falling in front of Miranda and her friends embarrassed him.

"I'm sorry," I say again.

But Aaron still doesn't answer me.

Now I'm the one who ruined Hanukkah.

CHAPTER 14

The New Story of Hanukkah

The sixth night of Hanukkah is pretty much the worst. Aaron takes a medicine that makes him sleepy. So at least I don't have to talk with him again. But I still feel bad. Really, really, really bad.

Dad and I don't even bother lighting the menorah. That feels wrong to me, but

I don't think I'd want to do it without Aaron.

I need to fix things. But how? I can't magically make Aaron's broken leg better.

Still, an idea pops into my head. A really good one! It gets bigger and bigger until I think I might burst from all the excitement.

First, I gather up my art supplies. Then I get to work.

As a Hanukkah present to Aaron, I draw a comic book: *Aaron Friedman and the New Story of Hanukkah*. This story isn't about the Maccabees. It's about Aaron and me and the fun things we did this week. I fill up pages and pages with drawings. Our family lights the menorah on the very first night. Aaron shows me how to spin a dreidel while Cookie gets ready to pounce. Aaron wins our race when we skate in the park. (But I don't draw the part where he fell.)

I draw quickly, so maybe my work isn't the neatest thing ever. But a few hours later, I'm done. Now I need to give it to Aaron. I staple the pages together and slip the book under his door.

Hopefully it's enough.

The next morning, Aaron wakes up really late. His crutches clang loudly while he walks down the stairs.

Aaron sags into the couch and pulls his broken leg up so that it lies flat.

"Did you get your present?" I blurt out.

He actually smiles at me! "Yep," he says. "I got it."

That's a good sign. It has to be. I start to feel a whole lot better.

"I really am sorry that you got hurt," I tell him. "And also that I embarrassed you in front of the girl you like."

Aaron squishes his face up like he has a question.

"How did you know I like Miranda?" he asks.

"Dad told me."

He rolls his eyes. "I guess Dad can read minds. And also he has a big mouth."

I agree about both of those things. But Aaron still hasn't accepted my apology. Does that mean it isn't good enough?

"Are you mad at me?" I ask.

Aaron moves his leg a bit and looks up

99

at me. "How can I be mad at you when you made me the star of my very own comic book?"

I bounce in place. "You read the whole thing?"

"Duh. It was pretty good."

Coming from Aaron, that means my comic was great! I feel way, way better about everything. Like maybe I didn't totally and completely ruin Hanukkah.

"'A long, long time ago, the Maccabees fought a war, and there was a miracle and stuff,'" Aaron says. That's exactly what I wrote at the beginning of my comic! He remembers it! "'But this isn't a story about that. This is another story about Hanukkah.' Pretty good stuff, Rachey!"

"I thought so, too!"

Aaron snorts. "Well, don't start to get

too much of a big head or anything. But I
liked it."

"Thank you," I say. Because I am very
polite. I don't mean to say anything else, but
I start speaking again. "I just wish it could
have been a better Hanukkah, you know? I
really, really wanted this Hanukkah to be

perfect. I even made a list, but . . . things went wrong. Really, really wrong."

Aaron sits up straighter on the couch. "What's this about a list?" he asks.

So I explain everything to him. About Mason and what he said. The list I made with Maya. And how absolutely nothing has gone the way I wanted it to.

For once, Aaron listens to me without interrupting a single time. But when I'm done, he shakes his head. "No offense, Rachey, but that is probably the stupidest thing you have ever told me."

And here I thought he was being nice to me! I cross my arms and scowl at him.

"I am not stupid! I just wanted to prove that Hanukkah is the best holiday. I mean, what's so great about having a tree in your house, anyway?"

Aaron doesn't speak for a long, long

time. When he does, he uses his nice voice. For once.

"Why is it so important to prove that Hanukkah is better than Christmas?" he asks.

Huh. I would never tell him so, but Aaron asks very good questions. Almost too good. Why did I want to prove that Hanukkah is the best holiday?

I play with my hands. "Mason annoyed me so much! He shouldn't feel sorry for us because we don't do Christmas! Even though . . ."

I can't finish the sentence. I know what I want to say, but I can't say it out loud.

Aaron says it for me. "Even though maybe you sometimes wish we did celebrate Christmas? Just so you could know what all the fuss is about?"

I make a face. "Maybe. But isn't it bad to think that?"

My brother shrugs and waves a hand. "It's only a feeling. It is what it is. You still love being Jewish, right?"

"Of course!" That's never ever been a question for me.

"Then I don't think there's anything wrong with feeling a bit jealous about Christmas. I mean, things do get weird around this time of year. It's almost like everyone else keeps talking about a party you're not going to. And then they keep saying you should go to the party even when you explain that you can't."

"Yes! It's exactly like that," I tell him. Who knew that Aaron and I could agree on so many things?

"You're not wrong for how you feel," Aaron says. "But, you know, I don't think Christmas really is perfect for anyone. Even if it seems that way in all the movies and commercials. There's no such thing as a perfect holiday, you know?"

After this week, I definitely do. I sigh.

Well, at least Hanukkah isn't over yet. I look at my brother. Maybe, just maybe, he'll finally agree that Hanukkah is fun.

"Do you feel like doing something Hanukkah-y right now?" I ask him. "Maybe we can build the Lego menorah. You can sit down while doing that."

Aaron shakes his head. "Yeah, no. My friends are coming over to watch movies soon. And, before you ask, no, you're not invited. These are *grown-up* movies."

I start to protest that this is the most unfair thing ever. But Aaron is already hobbling out of the room on his crutches.

I'm still alone for Hanukkah.

CHAPTER 15

The Return of the Potatoes

After my talk with Aaron, I feel much better about everything. Maybe I haven't exactly had eight perfect days and eight perfect nights. And maybe I won't be able to finish everything on my list. But that doesn't mean the rest of Hanukkah can't be completely and totally fantabulous. The seventh night was good, and tonight's the eighth. It's the last night of Hanukkah, and I will make it count!

Even though Aaron said my list was stupid, I look at it anyway. Maybe I don't have to do every single thing on the list, but it does have some good ideas. When I look it over, I'm surprised to see that I've already done a bunch of things on it! Even if things didn't exactly go 100 percent according to plan. I'm even going to get the race car tonight. I know because I saw it in the back of the car trunk. So *that's* where Dad hides the presents!

Of course, there's still one thing on my list that I haven't done. And I really, really want to.

"Did you remember to get the potatoes?" I ask Dad in the afternoon.

I don't want to be annoying about this.

But, well, it's Hanukkah! We have to eat latkes on Hanukkah.

Dad smiles at me. "Yes, Rachel. I bought all the potatoes you could possibly want."

Yes! It's latke time!

Here's the thing about latkes: They take a really, really long time to make, and it's a whole lot of work. We start on the latkes an hour before dinner. Pretty soon, my hands are sore from peeling so many potatoes.

Aaron walks in with his crutches while I'm busy with the potatoes. He finds a seat by the table. For a moment he just sits there, and I narrow my eyes at him. I don't think it's fair for him to eat the latkes if he isn't going to help make them. But I guess he is still hurt, so I will try to be nice.

Then he surprises me.

"Do you need help?" Aaron asks. "I don't need two working legs to peel potatoes."

I toss a potato over to him, and he gets started. Everything goes much faster with three people instead of only two.

Even though I want to be nice to Aaron, I do have a question for him.

"Why are you here?" I ask.

He frowns at the bowl of potatoes. "Um, because it's Hanukkah?"

"I thought Hanukkah wasn't important!" I remind him. "You said you were too cool to build a Lego menorah or a Snow Maccabee! All week, you were too busy watching movies and reading to do Hanukkah stuff."

Aaron puts down the potato peeler with a frown. "Well. I guess I did think I was too old for Hanukkah stuff. Now that I'm thirteen and everything. But maybe I was wrong about that."

Dad raises an eyebrow and talks for the first time in a while. "Is that so?"

My brother makes a face, but he nods. "Yeah. I guess Hanukkah can be fun after all."

I can't help it. I smirk at him. In my

mind, I check off number eight on my list: *Get Aaron to admit that Hanukkah is fun.*

I start to say "I told you so," because I did tell him so. But before I get the chance, Cookie leaps up onto the table and starts sniffing around the potatoes.

"Cookie, NO!" Aaron and I say together.

I wag a finger at her. "Latkes are not for cats!"

So I have to go scoop her up and put her outside the kitchen. She meows. I think that means she doesn't like being left out.

Poor kitty! I'll have to make sure to include her in Hanukkah stuff later. Just not anything that involves food. Or candles. Or dreidels.

As I'm about to go

back to the kitchen, someone knocks on the door. I rush to open it. And there's the best surprise ever.

"Hiya, Rachel!" Maya says.

Yay, yay, and yay! My best friend is here, standing on the front porch with her moms. Plus, there's a big cardboard box in her hands.

I bounce over, wanting to hug her, but I stop because I don't want to squash whatever she's carrying. But I make lots of happy sounds as I let our visitors inside.

"Happy Hanukkah!" I tell them. "Did you have a good holiday?"

"I was sick," Maya reminds me. "But other than that, it was actually pretty good. My moms and I watched the *Rugrats* Hanukkah special! *And* I got a jewelry-making kit."

I notice a new bracelet on Maya's wrist, and I grin. That's another thing on the list checked off. Then I remember the mysterious box in her arms.

"What's in the box?" I ask.

"That would be the jelly doughnuts," one of Maya's moms says.

Yay again!

I show Maya's family into the kitchen

so they can put down the doughnuts. Soon they join my family in making latkes.

Looking around the room, I let out a big smile. No, it hasn't been a perfect Hanukkah. But it's been a good one.

After all, everything is better with latkes and doughnuts.

Acknowledgments

Many people helped me to bring this story to life. First, thank you to my editor Dana Chidiac, for her always-sharp editorial suggestions. I would also like to extend thanks to the rest of the team at Macmillan: Ann Marie Wong, Jean Feiwel, Valery Badio, Alexei Esikoff, Sarah Gomp-per, Abby Granata, Aurora Parlagreco, Chantal Gersch, Molly Ellis, Mary Van Akin, Mariel Dawson, and Jen Edwards.

Much thanks also to my wonderful

agent, Jennifer Laughran, and the entire team at Andrea Brown Literary Agency, including Bex Livermore.

Yet again, Genevieve Kote has created magical illustrations that perfectly encapsulate Rachel's spirit. Thank you for your brilliant work. I always smile widely when I look at it.

Thanks to Meera Trehan for reading one of the earliest drafts of this book and providing very helpful suggestions and encouragement. I also very much appreciate Rabbi Ruti Reagan, whose feedback helped to shape the book's themes.

As always, thank you to my family—Neil especially. I love you and I could not do this without you.

Finally, thank you to everyone who has read my stories over the years.

DON'T MISS
RACHEL FRIEDMAN'S
NEXT ADVENTURE

When Rachel's not cast as Queen Esther in the Purim play, she has to learn to let someone else be the star of the show.

2/11/2025